MARY OF MILE 18

STORY AND PICTURES BY ANN BLADES

TUNDRA BOOKS

First published in hardcover by Tundra Books, Montreal, 1971
First published in paperback by Tundra Books, Montreal, 1975
First published in this 30th anniversary edition by Tundra Books, Toronto, 2001

Published in Canada by Tundra Books,
481 University Avenue, Toronto, Ontario M5G 2E9

Published in the United States by Tundra Books of Northern New York,
P.O. Box 1030, Plattsburgh, New York 12901

Library of Congress Control Number: 2001087249

National Library of Canada Cataloguing in Publication Data

Blades, Ann, 1947-
  Mary of Mile 18

30th anniversary ed.
ISBN 0-88776-581-5

I. Title.

PS8553.L33M3 2001   jC813'.54   C2001-930268-1
PZ7.B535Ma 2001

We acknowledge the support of the Canada Council for the Arts and the Ontario Arts
Council for our publishing program.

We acknowledge the financial support of the Government of Canada through the Book
Publishing Industry Development Program for our publishing activities.

Design: Terri-Anne Fong

Printed in Hong Kong, China

1 2 3 4 5 6   06 05 04 03 02 01

For the children of

Mile 18

It is a cold winter in northern British Columbia. At the Bergen farm, snow has covered the ground since early November and it will not melt until May.

One clear night in February, the temperature drops to forty degrees below zero and the northern lights flash across the sky. Mary Bergen gets out of bed and goes to the window to watch and listen. She hears a crackling sound and smiles, excited. Mary likes to pretend that if she hears the music of the lights, the next day will bring something special.

In the morning, Mary wakes up happy. At first she can't think why. Then she remembers, and wonders what the day will bring. She pulls on her boots, hat, heavy coat, and mitts, and walks to the henhouse to feed the chickens.

One winter day is so much like the next. *What can happen?* Her mother is expecting a new baby, but it is not supposed to arrive for another month.

Mary feeds the chickens and starts back. Seeing the house in front of her reminds her of another special day, the day her father finished building it. He was so proud. When the family first moved to the farm, they lived in the shack where the grain is now kept. Before that, they lived in town, but Mary does not remember so far back.

Mary's mother has told her of the comforts of town: water taps, electricity, telephones, and television. Here, water is brought into the house a pail at a time; the sink rains into another pail, which is carried outside and emptied. The bathroom is an outhouse and the bathtub is a big bucket. The family has a transistor radio to listen to, but Mrs. Bergen gets lonely sometimes.

The closest neighbors are the Fehrs, and their farm is two miles away.

Mary sees her father near the barn. The Caterpillar was damaged yesterday, and he is trying to fix it. Every winter day when it does not snow, Mr. Bergen likes to clear a little more land. He uses the Cat to push the trees down and into piles.

When summer comes, all the family will pick roots, tearing them out of the earth with their hands so that the land can be planted.

"When we clear most of this land, the government will give us the deed to it," her father explained. "This is why we have moved north: so that we can have our own farm and live our own way."

Before he comes in for breakfast, Mr. Bergen puts a propane torch under the truck to warm the engine. It will take an hour to warm because last night was so cold.

Usually Mary likes this time, just before they set out for school. This morning, Mr. Bergen is playing with little Eva. Isaac and Jake are looking at a book from the class library. Sarah tries to get Mary to crayon with her, but Mary can't keep her mind on it. *What can happen today?* She is anxious to get to school.

Mrs. Bergen serves breakfast. After the new baby comes, the girls will help even more than now. They will do dishes, cook meals, make beds, and scrub floors. But they won't mind. A new baby is so exciting.

The radio is on. The weather report is: "Snow this afternoon. Clearing and colder towards evening."

Mr. Bergen goes out first and starts the engine. He lets it run for a while, then honks the horn. Mary, Sarah, Jake, and Isaac come out and crowd into the seat beside him. It is a tight squeeze, but it is also nice and warm.

Today the teacher, Mrs. Burns, has turned the oil heater on full, but the room is still so cold that the children sitting beside the windows keep their coats on and edge closer to the heater. At noontime, Sarah watches the class while Mrs. Burns goes to the back to have her lunch. At three o'clock, Mary helps dress the smaller children. She ties their scarves over their heads and across their faces to protect them from the cold.

Mary sighs as she pulls on her own overshoes. School is over for the day and still nothing special has happened.

In the truck on the way home, Mr. Bergen listens to the children talk about school, but does not talk himself. He is watching the road carefully. Snow is drifting and it is hard to see.

Just as they near their farm, another truck looms out of the blowing snow. Mr. Bergen steers quickly to the right to avoid an accident and his back wheels slide into the ditch.

As Mary watches her father jack up the truck and put chains on the rear tires, she thinks, *I hope* that's *not the special thing.*

Then, farther up the road to the house, Mary sees something in the snow and cries: "Look, a puppy!" She runs to him, kneels down, and the puppy licks her mitt.

Mary carries the pup to the truck. "Please, Father, can I keep him?"

Mr. Bergen shakes his head. "You know the rules. Our animals must work for us, or give us food."

Mary protests: "A dog can help – "

Mr. Bergen interrupts: "That isn't a regular dog. He's part wolf, and wolf pups are useless. Take him into the woods and leave him. Come on, the rest of you. Chores."

Sadly Mary goes off with the pup while the others go about their jobs. Jake goes to the woodpile, takes an ax, splits logs, and carries them – an armful at a time – into the house. Both the woodstove that Mrs. Bergen uses for cooking and the barrel heater that warms the house take a lot of wood. Sometimes, even when both are going, the house is chilly.

The pup snuggles into Mary's arms as she carries him into the woods. How she wishes she could keep him! "I would call you Wolf," she says.

It has stopped snowing, but the path is covered over and the trees seem to grow closer and closer together. If she goes too far from the road, she might not be able to find her way back. She puts the pup down to see what will happen. He runs around, excited, sniffing at the trees. She turns and walks away. He does not follow.

That was something special alright, Mary thinks, as she walks home, *but it didn't last for long.*

Near the house Isaac passes her on their horse, Mouse. A few years ago, Isaac and Jake rode Mouse to school and kept her in the barn behind the schoolhouse. But now Mouse has to wait until Isaac gets home to go for a run.

The house smells of fresh-baked bread as Mary enters. Her mother looks up from the stove.

"Where have you been, Mary? Sarah is waiting for you. I'm almost out of water."

Silently Mary bends down, takes two empty buckets standing near the door, and goes out.

Sarah has already filled her buckets with snow. Mary does the same, and the two girls carry the snow into the house and dump it into a big barrel. They wait for it to melt, then go out for more snow.

From the barrel comes all the water for drinking, cooking, and washing. Tomorrow Mrs. Bergen will wash clothes and Sarah will stay home to help, so the barrel must be full tonight. In spring and summer, it is much easier. A barrel catches rainwater from the roof, and the river is unfrozen. But in winter, all the water comes from snow. When the snow is dry and powdery like today, it takes many trips to fill the barrel.

Each time Mary goes out, she looks toward the woods. Her father comes out of the barn, where he has been feeding the pigs, and goes into the house. Isaac returns with Mouse. The pup is nowhere in sight.

The coal oil lamp is lit and Mary sits at the table staring at her reader. Mrs. Bergen is making supper. Mr. Bergen is cleaning his gun. The radio says another cold night, and Mary thinks about the pup.

Suddenly there is a sound outside the door, a low whimper. Mr. Bergen goes to the door and opens it. Mary cries: "It's little Wolf," and rushes to take the pup in her arms.

Mr. Bergen is angry. "Why are you encouraging him to stay around? Get your coat on and get rid of him so that he doesn't come back."

This time Mary walks nearly two miles to the Fehr farm. "Perhaps Mr. Fehr will let his children keep you," she says, putting Wolf down near the door. "Then I can see you sometimes."

As she runs home in the cold night, her toes and fingertips sting and the air burns her throat.

The family is at the supper table when she gets back. Her mother looks up and says: "We have your favorite supper tonight, Mary. Moose steak."

"I don't want to eat, Mother."

Mrs. Bergen starts to object, but Mr. Bergen stops her: "Let the girl go to bed without eating if she wants to." His voice is still angry. "She should not have asked to keep the animal. She knows the rules."

Mary gets into bed and buries her head in her pillow. *Why is he so angry?* she wonders. Then she remembers last fall, when Jake and Isaac begged their father for a gun of their own. He refused and got angry then, too. Her mother explained: "Your father gives you everything he can. When you ask for more, it hurts him to refuse. That is why he gets angry."

Mary lies thinking about this until she falls asleep.

That night, when everyone in the Bergen house is asleep, another kind of animal – a coyote – comes out of the woods. He sniffs at all the buildings, then stops at the henhouse. Silently he paws at the rope that holds the door shut, and the rope comes loose. The coyote pushes the door to enter the henhouse and get at the chickens.

Suddenly, a shrill screech goes up in the night.

Everyone in the Bergen house wakes up. Mr. Bergen throws his clothes on quickly, grabs his gun, and goes out.

The rest of the family get up and crowd around the window to see what is happening. All except Mary. She hears Isaac say, "It's just a coyote," and she tries to go back to sleep so that she won't have to think about little Wolf out in the woods.

Mr. Bergen sees the coyote in the bright light from the snow. He aims his gun and fires.

His first shot misses. The coyote turns, snarling, then quickly runs behind the henhouse. Mr. Bergen fires again, but the coyote takes off and disappears over the hill.

Mr. Bergen goes to the henhouse and looks inside to make sure the chickens are alright. Then he carefully ties the door tight. He is about to return to the house when he sees something at his feet.

It is the wolf pup, wagging his tail. "So it was you who warned us," Mr. Bergen says. He bends down, takes the puppy in his hands, and looks at him. "Tough little fellow, aren't you? Not afraid of cold or coyotes. Maybe you will earn your keep after all."

He carries the pup into the house. Mrs. Bergen has lit the oil lamp and everyone is waiting for him, except Mary.

The children get excited when they see the wolf pup. Mr. Bergen puts his finger to his lips as a sign for them to be silent. He goes to the bedroom.

Mary looks up as her father comes into the bedroom. He puts the wolf pup down on the bed. "This little fellow would like to get warm," he says.

Mary can hardly believe she is not dreaming as she takes little Wolf in her arms. "Can I keep him?" she asks.

"I suppose you can," her father answers gruffly.

In the doorway of the bedroom, Isaac and Jake and Sarah and Mrs. Bergen, holding Eva in her arms, are all standing watching and smiling.

AUTHOR'S NOTE

Mile 18 is a real place, but it has a new name. Mile 18 was called Buick Creek during the 1970s, and is now known as Buick. If you want to visit Buick, you drive north from Fort St. John for about fifty miles on the Alaska Highway and turn right on the road to Buick. After eighteen miles, you will come to the community that used to be called Mile 18 when Mary Bergen and her family lived there during the 1960s. If you would like to see it on a map, you can find Buick north of Fort St. John and east of the Alaska Highway.